CITY STREET

by Douglas Florian

 Greenwillow Books, New York

Pen and ink and watercolors
were used for the full-color art.
The text type is American Typewriter.

Copyright © 1990 by Douglas Florian
All rights reserved. No part of this book
may be reproduced or utilized in any form or
by any means, electronic or mechanical, including
photocopying, recording, or by any information
storage and retrieval system, without permission
in writing from the Publisher, Greenwillow Books,
a division of William Morrow & Company, Inc.,
105 Madison Avenue, New York, NY 10016.
Printed in Hong Kong by South China Printing Company (1988) Ltd.
First Edition   10 9 8 7 6 5 4 3 2 1

Library of Congress Cataloging-in-Publication Data
Florian, Douglas.
City street / Douglas Florian.
p.   cm.
Summary: Pictures and minimal text present life
on a city street, where skateboards roll,
pigeons fly, and traffic moves.
ISBN 0-686-09543-7. ISBN 0-688-09544-5 (lib. bdg.)
1. City and town life—Juvenile literature.
2. Streets—Juvenile literature.
[1. City and town life—Pictorial works.
2. Streets—Pictorial works.]   I. Title.
HT151.F56 1990   307.3'362—dc20   89-28694   CIP   AC

For Diane, Erica, and Elena

4

City street

Jumping feet

Bus stop

PLAY
STREET

Skateboards roll

14

Hockey goal

City flowers

City showers

Sidewalk scrawls

Basketballs

Brownstone stoop

Pigeon coop

27

Twilight

City night